W9-BLL-407

REDWOOD
LIBRARY

THE WHITE STAG

Kate Seredy

Newbery Award Book

Those who want to hear the voice of pagan gods in wind and thunder, who want to see fairies dance in the moonlight, who can believe that faith can move mountains, can follow the thread on the pages of this book. It is a fragile thread; it cannot bear the weight of facts and dates.

Here is the epic story of the migration of the Huns and Magyars from Asia to Europe, written in beautiful, rhythmic prose, with pictures that reflect the breathtaking pageantry of history.

THE WHITE STAG

WRITTEN AND ILLUSTRATED

BY KATE SEREDY

PUFFIN BOOKS

PUFFIN BOOKS
Published by the Penguin Group
Penguin Books USA Inc., 375 Hudson Street, New York, New York 10014, U.S.A.
Penguin Books Ltd, 27 Wrights Lane, London W8 5TZ, England
Penguin Books Australia Ltd, Ringwood, Victoria, Australia
Penguin Books Canada Ltd, 10 Alcorn Avenue, Toronto, Ontario, Canada M4V 3B2
Penguin Books (N.Z.) Ltd, 182–190 Wairau Road, Auckland 10, New Zealand

Penguin Books Ltd, Registered Offices: Harmondsworth, Middlesex, England

First published by The Viking Press 1937
Published in Puffin Books 1979

40

Library of Congress Cataloging in Publication Data
Seredy, Kate. The white stag.
Summary: Retells the legendary story of the Huns' and
Magyars' long migration from Asia to Europe, where
they hope to find a permanent home.
1. Legends, Hungarian. [1. Folklore–Hungary.
2. Hungary–Fiction] I. Title.
PZ8.1.S457Wh 1979 398.2'1'09439 79-17074 ISBN 0-14-03.1258-7

Printed in the United States of America

TO MY MOTHER

FOREWORD

NOT so long ago I was leafing through a very modern book on Hungarian history. It was a typical twentieth-century book, its pages an unending chain of FACTS, FACTS, FACTS as irrefutable, logical, and as hard as the learned pens of learned historians could make them.

Turning the pages I felt as if I were walking in a typical twentieth-century city, a city laid out in measured blocks, glaring with the merciless white light of knowledge, its streets smooth, hard concrete facts. One could not stumble on streets like that, nor could one ever get lost; every corner is so plainly marked with dates.

My eyes fell on a paragraph:

"The early history of the Hungarian (Magyar) race is a matter of learned dispute. Their own traditions declare them to be descendants of the horde which sent forth the Huns from Asia in the fourth century. Our present knowledge of the history and distribution of the Huns tends to disprove this theory."

Well, I closed the book and I closed my eyes. And then I saw an old garden, the great, neglected park of old Hun-Magyar legends, with moss creeping over the shadowy paths, paths which twisted and turned, which led into hidden nooks where fantastic flowers grew around crumbling monuments of pagan gods.

And I saw a little girl and her father, tiptoeing along those winding paths, trailing the White Stag, gazing breathlessly into the circle of birch trees where Moonmaidens danced on a carpet of flowers, standing awed and still before the tomb of Nimrod, Mighty Hunter before the Lord, and bowing their heads to the great, crumbling stone altar of Hadur, Powerful God of Huns and Magyars. Often a path ended abruptly where a gigantic tree had crashed to the ground, its torn branches entwined in the creeping vines of centuries; but always the White Stag appeared to show them a new path.

It was beautiful, that park of legends, and the little girl who was I, had never forgotten it.

And now, thirty years later I went back again to walk those winding paths, to listen to the scream of the eagles, to pay homage to a race of brave men, men whose faith in their own destiny had led them to a land they still call their own. I went back but this time I walked alone. And I took a ball of golden thread with me and unwound it as I trailed the White Stag of legends from the great tomb of Nimrod to the green plains between two blue rivers—the Hungarian Plains.

Those who want to hear the voice of pagan gods in wind and thunder, who want to see fairies dance in the moonlight, who can believe that faith can move mountains, can follow the thread on the pages of this book. It is a fragile thread; it cannot bear the weight of facts and dates.

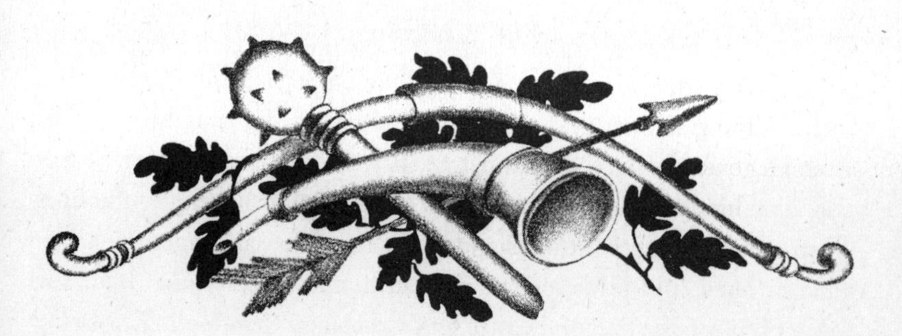

PART ONE

NIMROD, THE MIGHTY HUNTER

OLD Nimrod, Mighty Hunter before the Lord, leaned wearily against the stones of the sacrificial altar. There was sadness in his face, dejection in the stoop of his broad shoulders. The altar stones were cold to his touch; many a sun had set since the tribe could pay tribute to Hadur, their powerful God. Sheep and cattle had died of a strange ailment, game had deserted forest and field; there was nothing to offer on the altar.

Once in a while he lifted his bowed head and looked around, his eyes searching the paths among the trees, his ears tuned to catch the slightest noise. Nothing stirred—silence hung heavy in the air. Then he would bow his head again and remain motionless, lost in thought for a long time. The formidable, snowcapped mountains around the altar place looked down on him in supreme indifference. They knew him as he knew them; he had hunted their thickly wooded slopes almost all his life. He knew that beyond these mountains were others, peak upon peak, steep, cold, almost impassable, an army of hostile mountains. Now he remembered the years of struggle and suffering while he had crossed them, leading his people . . . always following the sun from east to west. He remembered the years before that, the happy years when he was young and strong and heedless, son of Cush the Great Leader; the time when all people were brothers and spoke the same language; the years, when in their vain pride, people wanted to reach heaven and built the tower of Babel; the dreadful day of terror, when for their foolhardy daring they were punished—when brother ceased to understand brother, when the terrific storm came and scattered them all over the earth like so many dry leaves scattered by the wind.

After the storm he and a handful of his people found themselves in a strange land—cold, rocky, barren. For a long, long time they suffered from cold and hunger, and then came the day when he again heard the voice of God, thunder, and was given the power to understand it. He knew from then on what he had to do.

Somewhere there was a land, rich in game and green pastures between two great rivers plentiful in fish, surrounded by mountains, warmed by the sun, sheltered from the cold; and this place would be the home of his people if he could lead them wisely from east to west, always following the sun to the promised land. Many a time he thought that they had found this land but each time Hadur spoke again and he led his people farther toward the west. Now he was old and soon the time would come when younger leaders would be needed. The tribe had grown until their numbers were as many as there were stars in the sky. They were strong and fearless, not a weakling among them. They would follow only the strongest, most fearless of leaders, one who could bend their recklessness to his will and bow his head to no one, only Hadur the Powerful God.

There were two such men in the tribe, two brothers, sons of Old Nimrod, Hunor and Magyar. They could ride faster, shoot straighter, fight harder than any other man. They could read the signs of sun, moon, fire and water. They would lead the tribe toward the promised land, for they, too, understood the voice of Hadur when it spoke in the wind and in thunder.

Old Nimrod lifted his head again to scan the darkening forest around him. He was waiting for his sons this evening as he had waited for them every day at sunset since they rode away, seven moons ago, to follow a stag, a miraculous White Stag. It had appeared one day at sunset, on the edge of the forest near the altar place. No one else had seen it only Nimrod and his sons. No one else had seen it, outlined against the western sky, with the red setting sun shining through its majestic antlers, almost as if it were supporting the sun. Hunor and Magyar had ridden off to capture it, leaving Old Nimrod behind for he was too old for a long hunt. Since then he had been waiting every day at sunset for their return.

Now, as the red sun touched the rim of the mountains, Nimrod turned to the altar and lifting his arms, sighed in prayer:

"O Powerful Hadur, have pity on me and my people. They are suffering with hunger; I am suffering with shame, for I have nothing to offer Thee; give me a sign to show me what I can do to appease Thy anger."

The silence was broken by a soft, neighing sound. Something cool and moist touched his arm. Taltos, his horse, faithful friend and companion of many great hunts, had come up to him silently and stood close now, his whole body trembling. Old Nimrod looked at the beautiful animal for a long time. Slowly two large tears rolled down his cheeks.

"So I must make an offering . . . the greatest sacrifice is wanted by

Thee, Hadur," he sighed. With tender hands he patted the trembling animal's neck, then turned away quickly and lighted the sacrificial fire on the altar. Smoke billowed and hung sluggishly in the still air. When the red flames licked through small kindling and caught the heavy logs, he led the horse up on the altar steps. For one long moment man and beast looked at each other. Then, with a great broken sob Old Nimrod grasped his heavy war-club and gathering all his strength brought it down on the animal's forehead. The horse fell without a sound. Old Nimrod crumpled on his knees. He bent lower and lower until his head touched the ground.

For a long time only the sharp crackling of burning wood broke the silence. Flames rose higher and higher. The crackling was submerged in the increasing roar of the fire. The sound grew and other sounds mingled with it: howls of wind which sprang from nowhere, rushing of water, thundering hoofbeats, screams of horses, cries of men and women.

Old Nimrod staggered to his feet and looked around with dazed eyes. From the camping ground his people were running toward him, stumbling, falling, pushed by a terrific gale. Tents were torn from their moorings and carried away. Horses had broken loose; they ran around wild-eyed and screaming. Sparks and flames of the fire had been blown into the grass around the altar and were burning a broad path toward the mountains, a clear-cut path, a highway of leaping roaring fire toward the west. Now thunder, frightening, long-drawn-out, deafening thunder, added its voice to the tumult. The ground shook as it reached its climax with a terrific crash. People fell on the ground and lay trembling, too frightened to cry out. Only Old Nimrod remained standing, a tall majestic figure, with his arms stretched straight up to the angry sky.

"Speak, O Powerful Hadur—speak to Thy servant!" he cried. Another thunder shook the ground and a third. After that came silence, so sudden and so deep that it was more terrifying than the storm before. The wind ceased as suddenly as it had come and the smoke rose once more straight into the air. Only the path of fire crept slowly westward, burning high and bright. Then a new sound, a scream piercing and high, rent the silence. It was the scream of an eagle, so shrill, so imperious, that everyone looked up in wonder. They saw a great eagle, holy bird of Hadur, circling slowly over the column of smoke. It cried again and hovered for a moment, suspended motionless on its giant wings. Then it plunged headlong into the fire. A gasp of horror rose from the people, but Old Nimrod said:

"Have no fear, my people. Hadur is speaking. Behold!" Where one eagle had been before, two more were circling. They flew side by side, their great wings touching, circled three times and flew off, one to the west, one to the north. Another eagle appeared as if it had taken shape from the smoke, circled around seven times and disappeared to give place to still another, a giant bird, greatest of all. Its tremendous wings caught the glow from the fire; they seemed red as blood. Its voice rose into a piercing, victorious cry as it soared higher and higher and finally flew in a straight line toward the west.

Old Nimrod followed its flight with his eyes until it was no bigger than a speck of dust in the sky. Then he turned to his people and said:

"Hadur has spoken. Listen to me, brothers. The first eagle told us that I, your leader for so many years, shall not be with you for long. I shall soon leave to go to the land of my fathers. My place will be taken by two leaders, Hunor and Magyar. They will lead you nearer the promised land but they shall not see it. After they are gone, there shall be another leader and it will be his son, greatest of all, with the mighty voice and wings red as blood, who will lead you into the promised land. His power will be so great that the earth will tremble and stars fall down at his approach. His warriors will be more than the grains of sand or blades of grass on the plains. Under the hoofs of their horses the ground will groan and the air will echo the clanking of their countless swords. He will be called the Scourge of Hadur, for nothing can resist his ruthless progress into the land of his destiny. The Scourge of Hadur, greatest of all warriors, Attila. Hadur has spoken. We will obey."

"Hadur has spoken—we will obey," repeated the listeners in a low murmur. Then the clear voice of a child rang out:

"But where are Hunor and Magyar? They went away seven moons ago!"

"They are coming back soon," answered Nimrod. "They are . . ."

"Coming NOW!" cried the child, pointing to the west.

Two riders appeared on the crest of the hill and rode swiftly nearer, skirting the path of fire. They rode side by side, their spurred boots touching. Their saddles were laden with game, their faces proud and happy.

"Twin Eagles of Hadur," whispered a woman. The crowd stirred in excitement. People repeated the women's words first in puzzled whispers, then in a great, joyous shout: "Hunor and Magyar . . . Twin Eagles of Hadur! Welcome!"

Hunor and Magyar leapt from their saddles and ran to Old Nimrod. He embraced them silently. After a moment Hunor lifted his head and looked intently into his father's face.

"Father . . . you are pale and trembling. What has happened?" He made a sweeping gesture with his hand. "The people here . . . the path of fire . . . it met us far, far beyond the hills. Tell us the meaning of it."

Old Nimrod smiled. "I will tell you, my son. But I see that you have had a good hunt, you have brought game. Our people are hungry—let us have a feast."

At his signal men sprang forward and unloaded the game from the saddles. Soon huge fires were burning and the smell of roasting meat—of deer wild boar, and rabbits—filled the air.

The worst pangs of hunger appeased, people began to sing and laugh. By the time the full round moon sailed into view, it looked down on a happy boisterous scene. Hunger and terror were forgotten once more. Young men of the tribe were dancing around the fire, the wild dance of Lucky Hunters. Women sang and children scampered around like bouncing rabbits.

Only Old Nimrod was quiet and thoughtful. He had not touched food or drink but listened intently to the talk of Hunor and Magyar and answered their eager questions. When finally the merrymaking passed its peak, he walked slowly up the altar steps. He held up his hand, commanding silence. Then he began to speak:

"My people—you have seen the sun set on a day so portentous that it will be remembered long after we, who have been part of it, are dust and ashes. Before the Pale White Sister of the sun disappears behind the mountains, you will swear obedience to your new leaders, Hunor and Magyar. It is seldom that Hadur the Powerful speaks as clearly as he has spoken tonight, so clearly that even a child can understand His words. All of you have seen and heard and all of you will obey. There is one more thing you must know. Hunor and Magyar will tell you the story of their travels of seven moons. It is the final proof that they were chosen to be your leaders."

His two sons stepped up and stood by his side. They were very tall and powerful but Old Nimrod towered over them as a majestic old oak towers over young saplings. At the sight of the three gigantic figures illuminated by the pale white light of the moon a murmur of awe rose from the crowd. Then Hunor began his story:

"Seven moons ago a miraculous White Stag appeared on the crest of the hill. He was white as the driven snow and bigger than any stag ever seen by man. He waited until we were so close to him that we thought we could touch him with our hands, then he spun around and leaped away as lightly as sunlight leaps over running water. His legs were slim as the branches of white birch and he ran swifter than the wind.

"All night he ran through forests and plains across rivers and over mountains, and we rode after him as we had never ridden before. The hoofs of our horses never touched the ground, we soared over valleys and left mountains far below us. When morning came the White Stag stopped on the edge of a misty blue lake. As he stopped, our horses fell back exhausted, they stumbled and snorted and would not move again. The White Stag pawed the ground where he stood and shook his antlers, then he disappeared in the floating mist over the water.

"All that day we searched for him. We did not see him again. We only found the place where he had pawed the ground. There were seven deep rifts in the ground, cut deep and wide as no living beast could cut them. And we saw that the blue lake was full of fish, the green meadows alive with rabbits, the forests around it teeming with deer and other big game.

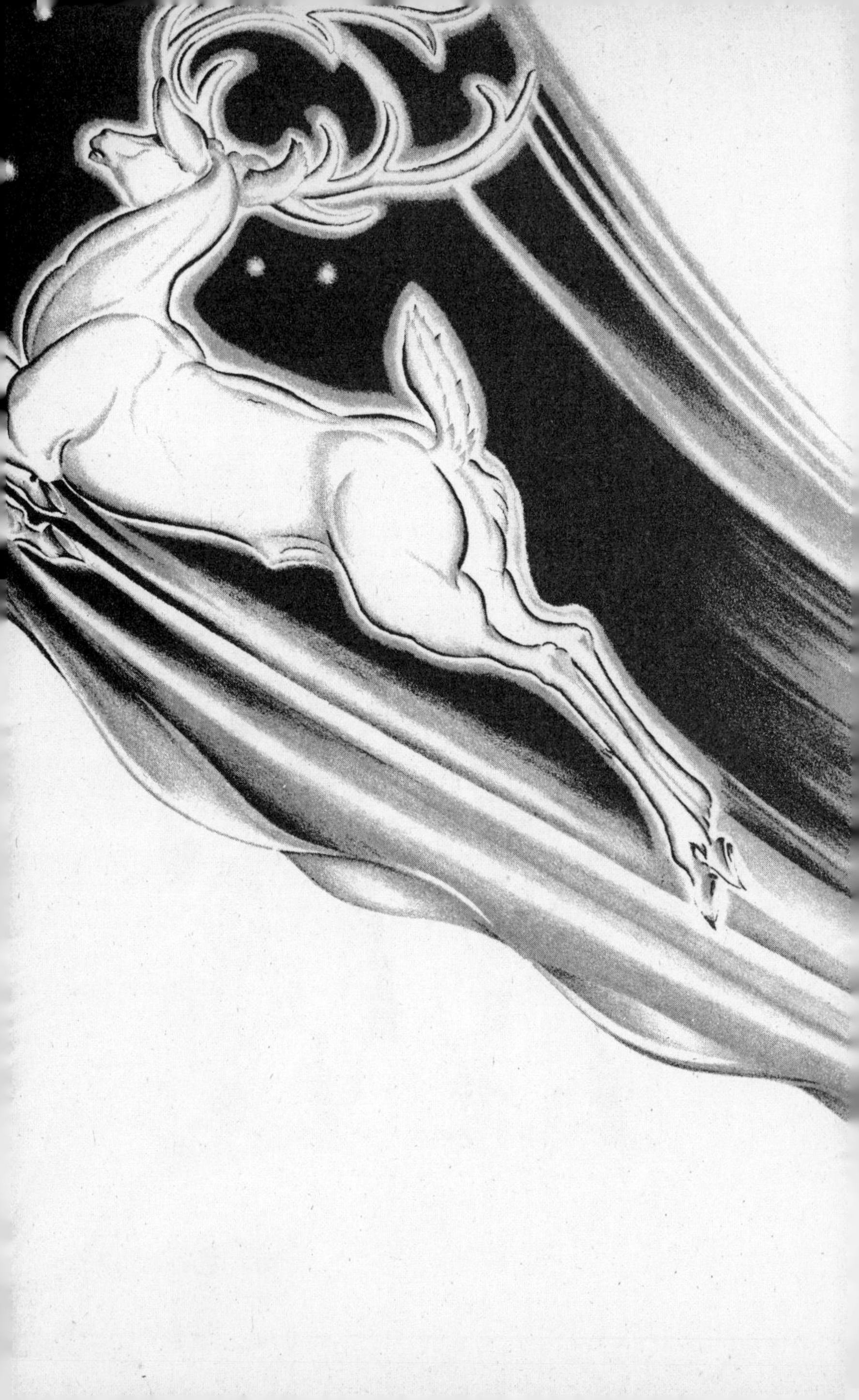

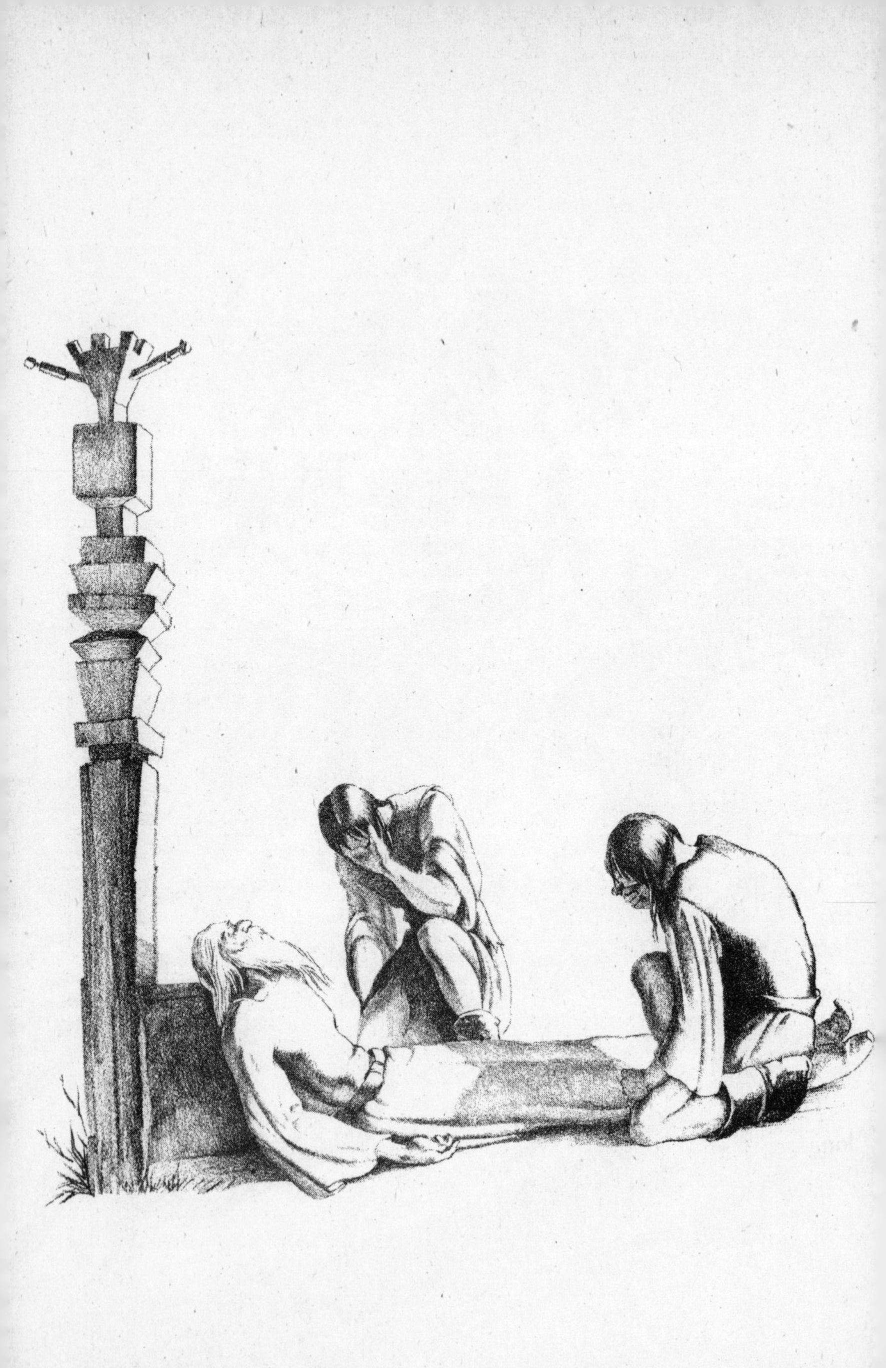

There were trees heavy with fruit and the air was sweet with the breath of beautiful flowers. We saw that in that land there would be room and food for all of us.

"We rested there for a short time, then started back. The White Stag had led us there in one night. . . . It took us seven moons to come back again."

While Hunor told his story, the listeners had left their fires and crowded closer and closer until they were standing in a tight ring around the altar.

Now Old Nimrod mounted to the very highest step, so close to the still smoking glowing embers that he seemed enveloped in a red mist. His face was pale and haggard and there was a far-seeing piercing look in his eyes. In one hand he held his war-club, in the other his bow and arrow. These he held out to his sons who, kneeling before him, took them from his hands. Then he spoke:

"My work is done. Tomorrow you will go forth to lead your people toward the promised land. Twin Eagles of Hadur—Hunor and Magyar—go and fulfill the will of God."

His eyes closed as he uttered these last words. Then, with a crash like that of a fallen tree, he fell on the highest step of the altar.

The crowd gasped in horror, women wailed, and children started to cry. But sounds of horror and mourning were drowned by a tremendous shout from the young warriors and hunters:

"Long live Hunor and Magyar, Twin Eagles of Hadur!"

The two brothers remained kneeling by their dead father's side for long minutes. Then they arose. Magyar turned to the tribe.

"Light the torches of the Dead," he commanded. One by one the warriors stepped to the dying embers and lighted pitch-coated torches. Soon there were hundreds of them burning around the altar. The whole valley seemed aflame once more and black smoke coiled upward, blotting out the sky. Hunor and Magyar, each with a burning torch, stood by the body of Nimrod. Hunor then lifted his voice:

"Light up the world, my torch! Shine brighter, O Moon, Stars, and Sun! Hold a wake over Nimrod, Mighty Hunter before the Lord!

"Shed bitter tears, O clouds, soil, trees, and grass—shed bitter tears for Nimrod, Mighty Hunter before the Lord.

"Bow your heads, all you living, bow your heads to Nimrod, Mighty Hunter before the Lord.

"Then cheer and dance and rejoice, all you living. Shine brighter, Moon, Stars, and Sun. Cry tears of joy, clouds, soil, trees, and grass.

"For now he is soaring over the Happy Meadows, for he is not taking shame but glory to lay before Hadur the Powerful God."

Every one repeated:

"He is taking not shame but glory to lay before Hadur the Powerful God."

Now Hunor and Magyar fastened their torches to the altar stones, all others were extinguished. Magyar stepped forward and cried:

"Move the mountains, men! Move the rocks and the soil with your bare hands to build a mighty tomb for the Mighty Hunter!"

In the eerie light of white moon and flickering torches the immense task began. Men tore bowlders from the mountainside and rolled them to the altar. Women and children carried clay from the river in their hands. Rocks were fitted together with the clay until they formed a gigantic mound over the altar; a mound shaped like an inverted cup,

tapering toward the top and hollow inside. Finally there was only a small opening on the top through which the glow and smoke of the torches poured.

Only then did Hunor speak again:

"Go and rest, brothers, until the sun comes up. With the sun we shall go forth toward the west."

The two brothers were left alone. They stayed by their father's grave for the rest of the night, watching the moon go down behind the hills, watching the first faint glow of a new day in the easterly sky. With the growing light came sounds of the awakening camp. Magyar roused himself out of his deep thoughts and touched his brother's shoulder:

"The tribe is ready; we must go now."

The women came first, leading the children. Every one had a flower in her hand. Silently they passed by the grave and dropped their flowers at its base. The men came next, leading their horses. Every one stopped to place a gift on the grave—an arrow, a wooden cup, a leather pouch, a favorite club. All passed and slowly the caravan began to move westward, following the now blackened path of the fire.

Hunor then shouldered a big square rock and walked slowly, laboriously to the top of the mound. Magyar followed. They rolled the rock over the opening, sealing it. Then they lifted their hunting bugles to their lips. A proud, triumphant tune rent the still air and echoed from the mountains a thousandfold, until its voice seemed to beat against the very sky—a bugle call of victory in last tribute to Nimrod, Mighty Hunter before the Lord.

PART TWO

TWIN EAGLES OF HADUR

THE untamed wilderness closed on the broad path broken by fire and crushed by sharp hoofs of horses. Fresh green sprouts grew on charred roots, vines covered deserted camping grounds. Black bear and tawny mountain lion stalked their prey once more unmolested by hunters. Snow fell and the last traces of men were covered with a thick, white blanket. The people of Hunor and Magyar had left the headlands of wild Altain-Ula forever. The snowcapped peaks had looked at their coming and going with indifference; in twelve moons they had forgotten them. To the everlasting mountains they meant no more than the passing of dry leaves blown by the wind.

But the people had not forgotten the mountains, nor had they forgotten Old Nimrod. The memory of his strength was like an armor around them; their belief in Hadur like a magic sword nothing could resist. Wild beasts prowling in the wilderness, hostile spirits hovering in mountain caves, hot sun blistering the plains, roaring rivers, or howling blizzards were powerless against the tribe. Relentlessly they pressed on toward the promised land.

Hunor and Magyar became worthy successors to their father. They led the tribe safely to the gentle hills by the misty blue lake. For years they stayed there, undisturbed, gaining in strength and numbers.

In the most beautiful spot of the new land they built the altar. There fragrant herbs of the fields were burning day and night. There great festivals were held every spring when the ever-smoldering embers were stirred into roaring flames, when offerings of game and fruit were brought to Hadur. Then every man, woman, and child would gather and listen to the minstrels as they sang of the past and future. Old songs, wailing, sinister, like the voice of hostile spirits in the wilderness of Altain-Ula; new songs full of joy and laughter like the laughter of good fairies who lived by the misty blue lake; rousing songs full of faith, of the coming of Attila.

The story of the White Stag became a song too, a song every one knew by heart. And there was the silent question in every heart—would the White Stag come again to lead them toward the promised land?

Then one day Hunor and Magyar saw the White Stag again. They had been away all day on a hunt. Descending darkness found them still far away from camp. They spurred their horses on for it was not wise for any man to spend the ghost-hour in the woods. They rode as fast as they dared through the thick dark forest but the ghost-hour was upon them. Green-eyed owls, restless spirits of wicked men, hooted at them from the branches; wild cats snarled in the underbrush and lichens; hoofmarks of the Devil shimmered on old treestumps. Gray mist crawled from the damp ground blotting out paths and landmarks. The forest grew denser, trees blocked the paths, brambles tore at them, hanging vines caught at them.

Hunor and Magyar reined in their trembling horses and peered around, trying to penetrate the darkness. They knew that they were lost in this strange, ghostly forest. Suddenly Hunor exclaimed:

"Look, brother, to your right . . . the White Stag!"

Shimmering white against the dark trees stood the stag not far away. He seemed to float on the rolling mist, to move with it slowly, silently away.

"Follow him!" whispered Magyar and his words echoed from the trees in the suddenly friendly forest: "Follow him!"

"Follow him," whispered the leaves.

"Follow him," gurgled a hidden spring.

"Follow him," sighed the wind.

Thorny branches coiled out of the way and vines crept back to let them through. Always in sight but never letting them nearer moved the White Stag silently. Trees fell behind, now they were riding on a grassy hill. A brook tinkled like silver bells and the breeze sang sweeter than the flutes of minstrels. A cluster of white birches gleamed at the top of the hill. There the White Stag turned to look at Hunor and Magyar, then they lost sight of him. When they reached the trees, he was nowhere in sight but the sound of bells and singing grew stronger. Now it seemed to come from the quivering silvery leaves of birches, such a lilting luring magic sound, that they stopped to listen.

"Do you hear laughter and singing, brother?" asked Hunor.

"Do you see fairies dancing, brother?" asked Magyar.

As if their questions had drawn a veil from their eyes, an enchanting scene opened before them. The white birch trees formed a ring enclosing a smooth green carpet of grass and flowers. Dancing in this ring were two beautiful maidens, fair as none whom Hunor and Magyar had ever seen before. Their long hair was pale gold like the new moon. They wore wreaths of flowers in their hair and were clad in pure white garments. All around under the trees sat gay little dark men, coaxing sweet music out of their reed pipes.

The eyes of Hunor and Magyar flashed together.

"Moonmaidens," whispered Magyar.

Moonmaidens, those strange changeling fairies who lived in white birch trees and were never seen in the daylight; Moonmaidens who, if caught by the gray-hour of dawn, could never go back to fairyland again; Moonmaidens, who brought good luck to men.

"We must detain them. The ghost-hour is waning," whispered Hunor.

Silently they dismounted and tiptoed closer to the dancing fairies. They were inside the ring of trees when a shivering sigh went through the branches and the music stopped abruptly. Somewhere a cock crowed. The two fairies stood motionless in the ring, gazing at Hunor and Magyar with frightened eyes. A scurrying, scampering sound came from the underbrush. Where the little dark musicians had been a moment ago, were only gnarled roots and dead stumps of trees.

The two brothers smiled at the maidens and spoke to them gently. Hunor held out his hand; one of the maidens touched it with her fingers. Her touch was cool and light as if a bird's wing had brushed his hand. She turned to her sister and said something in a strange language. Now they seemed to have lost their fear because they smiled and let Hunor and

Magyar lead them to the horses. At the sight of the animals they gave a little surprised laugh and exclaimed with joy when they were lifted into the saddle.

The first rays of the sun cut a shimmering path through the trees. In the distance Hunor and Magyar could see the dark blue of the lake and pale blue of thin columns of smoke rising from many campfires. A lark shot into the air and burst into song, white daisies and blue cornflowers opened sleepy eyes to smile at them as they passed, a belated whippoorwill ran with them, hidden in the tall grass, crying:

"Here they come . . . here they come."

Near the camp a young boy jumped from the bushes and ran ahead on the path, crying:

"Here they come!"

People ran from tents and campfires, excited, happy, eager, crying:

"Moonmaidens! Hunor and Magyar have captured Moonmaidens."

They were surrounded, exclaimed over, marveled at. The story of how they found the maidens had to be told.

Only the boy, who saw them coming, was suddenly quiet. He stood apart from the crowd, motionless, rigid, gazing ahead with wide-open eyes, his face very pale. Hunor noticed the boy. He walked over to him and laid his hand gently on his head.

"Why do you look at us so strangely, Damos?" he asked. The boy pointed a shaking finger at the Moonmaidens.

"The white herons . . . I saw them last night." His voice was hardly more than a whisper yet it brought a hush over the crowd. People became serious and a woman exclaimed:

"He dreamed strange dreams last night, I heard him moan." She ran to the boy. "Tell us about your dream, my son." Damos shook his head.

"It was not a dream, Mother—I was not asleep."

"What did you see, Damos? Tell us," urged Hunor. The boy began to speak haltingly in a low voice:

"Last night I went to sleep in my mother's tent. I don't know how long I had slept when I felt someone touch my eyes and I heard a call: 'Damos! Damos! Wake up and see. See and remember. Remember and speak.' I opened my eyes. There was no one in the tent and it was very dark outside. I heard the call again, then I went out. There was a light by the altar and I saw an old man standing on the steps. I have seen him before some place but I cannot remember when or where. He was very tall—taller than Hunor, taller than Magyar. His hair was long and white and his eyes"—the boy faltered for a moment, then his voice grew stronger—"he . . . CALLED me with his eyes! He called me and I went to him. He spoke to me again but his voice was not the voice of a man. It came from the ground and the sky. It came from the trees and stones and from my own heart, it came from everywhere."

"Nimrod!" groaned someone in the crowd. "His voice was like that."

The boy went on:

"The voice said: 'Open your eyes, Damos, and see. See and remember.' I saw the embers on the altar glow brighter. I saw flames lick higher and higher, slim narrow flames, pointed like swords. I followed them with my eyes and then I saw . . . I saw two great eagles flying above. Between them flew two white herons, whiter than snow and slim, beautiful to behold. For a long time they flew together, then I lost sight of them. Again I heard the voice: 'See, Damos, and remember.'

"I saw one eagle and one white heron and then they seemed to merge

together until there was only one white bird, a white eagle. I heard the voice: 'Hear, Damos! See, Damos! See, hear, and remember!'

"I heard the clash of swords and the whine of flying arrows, I heard thundering hoofbeats and the battle-cry of warriors. I saw the white eagle change color . . . become red . . . red as blood. He swooped down, down, until his talons touched the flames and soared up again with a flaming sword clutched in his claws. The voice roared from the ground and the sky, the stones and the trees: 'Damos! Remember and speak!' "

The boy stopped. He was trembling like a leaf. As if the cloak of magic had fallen from him he stood there, just a frightened, tired little boy again. Once more he began in a whisper:

"I was frightened. Everything became dark and I ran, I ran I don't know where. When light came I saw Hunor and Magyar, the white herons perched on their shoulders. I cried: 'Here they come!' and suddenly"—his voice broke and he finished with a childish sob—"and suddenly there weren't any white herons, only pale-faced girls with yellow hair. And now I can't see anything." He stumbled forward, groping with his hands:

"Mother! Where are you?"

Hunor sprang forward and caught the boy in his arms. He looked into his eyes intently. Then he turned to the silent awed crowd:

"The child is blind. He has seen what no human eyes can see—the future—and its glare has blinded him. Do not grieve for him, for now we have a prophet, one who will warn us and guide us, one who like my father, Nimrod, saw the coming of Attila." He turned to the boy's mother. "Lead him to the tent and let him rest."

An old warrior spoke now:

"The boy saw more than that, Hunor. He saw the mating of Twin Eagles of Hadur with white herons—white herons or Moonmaidens?"

Now every one looked at the strange maidens. They were standing quietly under a tree, unfrightened, smiling and talking to each other; strange pale maidens with golden hair. Hunor and Magyar had brought them . . . the Twin Eagles of Hadur had found them . . . slim graceful maidens beautiful to behold, with their wispy white garments spread out like the wispy feathers of white herons or the rays of the pale moon. But they were warm and friendly like any human girl. White herons or Moonmaidens, fairies or humans, who were they? Who could tell?

In time the Moonmaidens ceased to be the cause for wonder and curiosity. From the day when Hunor and Magyar had brought them to the camp, children of the tribe followed them wherever they went; they were so beautiful and gay. Women of the tribe came to love them; they were so gentle and winning. Men respected them; they could heal the wounded and ease the sick. They learned to speak the language of the tribe and were called by the names Damos, the blind boy, gave them: Tünde and Cilla.

Damos was happy only when he was near Tünde. For hours he would sit by her side and listen to her singing.

"Her voice is as soft as the downy wings of a bird," he would say and then people remembered again his dream of white herons. He was held in respect and awe, for was he not given the power to see the future?

So it was Damos who lighted the Torch of Marriage for the wedding of Hunor and Tünde, of Magyar and Cilla. It was Damos who poured clear spring water on their hands, joined over the flaming torch. His eyes could not see them, but he could hear their simple sacred vows:

"Through fire and water I come to Thee, not fire nor water shall take me from Thee."

And it was Damos who, twelve moons later, carried Hunor's son up the altar steps and held him high for everyone to see. It was Damos who, on that day, named him Bendeguz, the White Eagle.

Fifteen years have passed. Fifteen peaceful years for the tribe by the misty blue lake. Young Bendeguz grew into a tall brawny boy, who could ride the wildest horses, who could shoot as straight and true as the best hunters. Boys of his age and even those who were much older soon accepted him as the best among them.

When he was ten years old the peaceful years for the tribe came to an end. A rainless windy spring was followed by a dry sultry summer. Green pastures turned a dusty brown, leaves hung limp on the drooping branches, fruit blackened and dropped shrunken to the ground. Day after day the sun came up a sullen red and flooded the valley with shimmering deadly heat. Springs ceased to flow and the water in the lake receded, leaving evil-smelling slime on its banks. Game deserted the stricken land, traveling toward the west in droves.

People grew gaunt and hollow-eyed, many of them became ill. They remembered the dark days in the wild mountains, the suffering, the starvation, and they knew that the time had come to move. No one questioned the command of Hunor and Magyar to pull up the tents, to prepare for a long journey. Old and young worked in the relentless heat and one day at dawn the caravan stood ready. But they were not one great united, but nameless tribe as when they had followed Hunor and Magyar out of the wilderness of Altain-Ula. In the long, peaceful years a slight, but gradually widening, rift had appeared in their once unbroken loyalty to the two brothers. The more reckless, adventurous among them looked for guidance to Hunor; Hunor who knew no fear and had no pity for the weak. Others loved the sober, gentle, serious Magyar. The birth of Bendeguz made the rift still deeper, until now both brothers had a following who would take command from no one but their own chosen leader. They called themselves Huns and Magyars now, and so they left the once happy fertile valley—still brother tribes united by one purpose and one belief, but ready to separate at the will of their leaders.

Hunor and Magyar were hardly aware of this. Twin Eagles of Hadur, they rode together, spurred boots touching, their eyes turned toward the promised land. Only at Hunor's side now rode his son, fierce fearless young Bendeguz. Often on the long journey he left his father's side to ride ahead—far, far ahead of the slowly moving caravan, his fair hair flying, his short white cape streaming out behind him in the wind like great wings. It was at these times that the words of Nimrod lived again in the hearts of old warriors:

"After Hunor and Magyar are gone, there shall be another leader and it will be HIS SON, greatest of all, with the mighty voice and wings red as blood, who will lead you into the promised land."

Here he was, trying out his wings, the White Eagle, Bendeguz.

PART THREE

WHITE EAGLE OF THE MOON

HUNOR and Magyar were prepared for a long journey into the unknown lands, but they could not foresee that this journey would last for many long years. They could not foresee that there was to be no more peace for their people until they had reached the land of their destiny. They did not know that when they had left the blue lake they had left the last unclaimed undefended land, had left Asu (Asia), the Land of the Rising Sun—and entered Ereb (Europe), the Land of the Setting Sun. They knew how to cope with wild beasts of the mountains or the occasional onslaught of marauding gangs, they were hardened to the burning heat and freezing winds of the plains, they knew how to pacify hostile spirits. But this time they encountered something that was stronger, more dangerous, than any of these: the desperate resistance of people who were defending their own lands. People who had found what the Huns and Magyars were seeking—a permanent home. If they ever needed the armor of belief and the sword of purpose, they needed them in these illimitable, tragic years; tragic for themselves because ensuing cruel wars changed their very souls, made fierce wild warriors of the once care-free hunters; and tragic for those who stood in their way, because they were crushed by a pitiless relentless torrent of savages. They swept across Scythia, leaving a path of destruction behind them; smoking ruins, desolate fields, and a multitude of the dead.

In vain did Magyar attempt to divert them toward the less populated north; the Huns, led by young Bendeguz, swept on. The wings of the White Eagle were stained with blood and his piercing cry was heard over the whole world.

For years there was no rest for them, there could be no rest. Like a sharp wedge they had driven themselves into Europe and now they were surrounded by enemies; they had to go on or perish. Not until Bendeguz was a grown man did they find a haven from the terrific storm they themselves had created.

On a narrow strip of land between the river Tanais (Don) and the river Rha (Volga) protected from the south by vast stretches of quicksand and brackish swamps, they found a stronghold where no enemy could surprise them. And once more tents were raised around an altar to Hadur. Once more men and women sat at peace around the campfires. But these were different tents and vastly different men and women. Tents were made of rich silks and velvets, filled with plundered treasures carried there by hundreds of captives. Their clothes were heavy with gold and precious stones, warriors were armed with swords and vicious sharp javelins. And the rift between Huns and Magyars had become a gulf that they could not bridge over if they tried. Here, in this haven of peace, the beauty of a slave girl and the coming of Attila severed the last thread that held the brother tribes together.

The Magyars were content to stay in this sheltered land but the Huns were restless. They had tasted battle and it was to their liking. Most restless among them was Bendeguz, who had tasted power over thousands of men. He knew that he only had to command and his warriors would go through fire or water, through danger and torture to carry out his wishes. But he knew that winter would be upon them soon, the many wounded had to be cared for, a tired army was sure to be defeated. So he used his power to hold his men in restraint, a hard task for him who wanted to go on more than any of them. At night he could not sleep—the sound of his charging army, the clashing of swords, and their wild shouts of victory echoed in his heart. He was like a caged eagle waiting for the day when he could spread his wings again.

One night he left his tent and rambled around aimlessly in the sleeping camp. He wandered to the enclosure where the captives' tents stood near the banks of the river Rha. The night was cold, silvery with moonlight, and silent; he could hear the river gently lapping against its banks. It was a sweet, soothing sound like the lullaby his mother used to sing. As he listened a change came into the rhythm of the river's song—now it was sad, yearning . . . and he could hear words. Someone was singing near by. The melody coiled around his heart and drew him, down the grassy slope, down to the river's edge he went. The soft grass deadened his footsteps and he saw the singer before she heard him. Leaning against a tree so close to the river that her moonlit figure was reflected in the water, stood one of the captive girls. Bendeguz stood motionless, watching and listening. Her deep sad voice seemed to melt the fierceness around his heart, the restlessness left him, he was at peace.

The song came to an end. The girl turned away from the river with a sigh . . . she saw Bendeguz. She made a move as if to run away, then shrank against the tree and faced him defiantly. There was contempt in her eyes and pride in the lift of her head. Bendeguz wanted to say: "Do not be afraid," but now he could not, for there was no fear in her eyes—just cold, proud contempt. He walked closer, he could have touched her, and still she faced him defiantly.

"What is your name?" he asked and his voice was gentle.

"Alleeta."

"Alleeta . . ." he repeated slowly, "Alleeta, your eyes are as cold as ice. Do you hate me?" She looked at him for a long time then she turned her head away.

"No, not now," she whispered. "Always I have before, but not now." She was speaking the language of the Huns, yet it wasn't the same. To Bendeguz the words she spoke were like her elusive reflection in the water, the same words he knew but subtly different. And suddenly the words of her song rang again in his ears:

Lead me westward,
White Eagle of the Moon, oh, lead me
On silvery rays of the Moon—
Westward I long to fly. . . .

"Alleeta, where did you learn that song—where did you learn the language of my people?" he asked. She looked at him, surprised.

"It is the language of my people and it is a song we all know, the Song of the White Eagle."

"The White Eagle!" exclaimed Bendeguz. "Who are you? Who are your people?" Alleeta lifted her head proudly. She stood like a white flame before him.

"I am the daughter of King Ashkenaz and my people are the Cimmerians, homeless wanderers upon the earth. Lost in the wilderness, downtrodden by the Scythians, slain by the enemy's swords, and torn by the fangs of famine for longer years than I can remember, we have never lost hope. We believed that some day we would find the land of peace, believed that some day the leader promised to us by our great forefather Gomer would come and lead us to that land—the leader who shall be called the White Eagle. And now we have been taken as slaves by you, Bendeguz, and hope is dead in our hearts. The White Eagle is but a song."

Bendeguz listened to her rushing words in silence. Then he said:

"Alleeta, do you know what my people call me?"

"Your name is Bendeguz—I know." He held out his hand to her.

"Alleeta, listen to me. My name is Bendeguz, the White Eagle! My people are also seeking a land of peace, promised to them by our forefather, Nimrod. We have been slain by swords and torn by famine on the way; now we kill and destroy not because we want to but because nothing must stand in our way, we must and we will reach the land of our destiny."

While he spoke these words, Alleeta came slowly closer to him and took his hand. He closed his strong fingers on her hand and went on:

"Tomorrow, Alleeta, your people shall be free. Tell them that they may leave us, or stay with us not as slaves but as our brothers. Tell them that our strength will be their strength, that we will never forsake them."

She had been looking into his eyes intently, searchingly. Now she smiled.

"I can speak for my people NOW, Bendeguz. I will follow wherever you go. We will follow the White Eagle of the Moon westward . . . always."

She stepped back and slipped away between the dark trees. She might have been a dream, but her voice floated back to Bendeguz, growing fainter and fainter:

Lead me westward,
White Eagle of the Moon, oh, lead me . . .

Bendeguz, back in his tent, was also singing softly:

On silvery rays of the Moon
Westward I long to fly . . .

And, as he drifted into sleep, his last thought was:

"Westward . . . but not alone, not alone any more."

Huns and Magyars rejoiced with their new found brothers, the Cimmerians, when Bendeguz and Alleeta announced their decision. The downtrodden, abused, enslaved Cimmerians could hardly believe that once more they were free, that they were equals, and more, they were brothers of the proud Huns. Hope again lived in their hearts and they accepted Bendeguz as their leader unquestioningly.

Their happiness seemed to have touched a gentle chord in the wild hearts of Hun warriors. For years they had known only hatred and defiance; to them the friendliness of these people was like cool water to a thirsty man. Their restlessness and their longing for action were diverted into a new channel; tirelessly they listened to the songs and tales of the Cimmerians. A strange turn of a phrase, a new tune, a good story, made them shout with mirth and admiration.

Proud, beautiful Alleeta captured the heart of every one. The day came when she and Bendeguz stood on the altar steps, their hands clasped over the flaming torch. Huns, Magyars, and Cimmerians, old and young, sick and well, waited with bowed heads while Damos, the blind prophet,

poured the water over their hands. They spoke the age-old vows:

"Through fire and water I come to Thee, not fire nor water shall take me from Thee."

And it was as if earth and sky had echoed these words as the thousands who had assembled around the altar repeated them. Quick tears of happiness sprang into Alleeta's eyes and she bowed her head humbly. For this was more than her own marriage; it was the union of two great tribes brought together by the will of the Lord.

Through her tears she watched the long procession of gift bearers, watched as the oldest warrior presented Bendeguz with the gift of the Huns—a large white flag—watched as Bendeguz unfurled it and let it flutter in the wind. Then, as she looked at the flag, the icy hand of fear gripped her for a moment and a small voice in her heart cried out against this symbol of the future. Painted on the snowy silk was a red eagle with its great wings spread wide, its cruel beak open, clutching a flaming sword in its talons. It fluttered behind her like a living thing, a ruthless bird of prey waiting . . . waiting.

But before her were thousands of her people, listening in silence for a word of approval, people who had given her their loyalty and love, her people and the people of Bendeguz, who were ready to give their lives, ready to go through suffering and death under this flag. She was one of them now, she must accept their fate.

Once more unafraid she faced the waiting crowd; proud brave beautiful Alleeta, wife of Bendeguz. Then she removed the golden belt of her gown and fastened it firmly to the flag, a silent pledge more eloquent than any words she might have spoken.

Soon came the coldest cruelest winter the Huns and Magyars had ever known. Snow lay thick on the ground for months and the icy northerly winds howled like malignant demons. When finally spring came, the thawing snow swelled the rivers into raging torrents impossible to cross. Unwonted idleness began to chafe the restless spirit of warriors. As spring passed into summer they became sullen, irritable. And still Bendeguz, for the first time in his life, stood undecided. He was torn between duty to his people and anxiety for his beloved Alleeta, for Alleeta was ill. Since the long, cruel winter she had been burning with a strange, slow fever which sapped her strength and left her pale and wan. He could not take her into the dangers waiting for them once they left this haven of safety.

This delay and the peaceful contentment of the Magyars became a challenge to the Huns; a contrary word, a rough jest would lead to ugly quarrels. Tenseness grew until the brother tribes stood on the brink of open enmity. In vain did old Magyar plead with the men; in vain did Hunor remind them of the happy days when the two tribes were truly brothers; in vain did Bendeguz punish those who again and again started these bitter wrangles. Suppress his warriors for a few days he could, but their resentment smoldered under his discipline as embers smolder under a thin blanket of ashes—a gust of wind, a careless word, and the fire of hatred would flame up again.

Bendeguz, in desperation, went to the remote tent where Damos the prophet spent his days. He found Damos deep in meditation. He waited until the prophet turned his sightless eyes toward him.

"Bendeguz, my great White Eagle," he said gently.

Bendeguz sank to his knees beside him and grasped his hands.

"Yes, Damos, it is Bendeguz . . . but not the great White Eagle, just a humble and deeply troubled man." Damos sighed.

"Has love made you weak and blind, Bendeguz? Has it taken the sword of Hadur out of your hand? Are you deaf to the call of your destiny?" Bendeguz bowed his head.

"Yes, Damos. I am blind, weak, and deaf. I have almost lost faith in that distant promised land. No, wait!" he cried as Damos shook him off and sprang to his feet. "Wait, Damos! Listen to me. Our brothers, the Magyars, are content to stay here on this sheltered land between two great rivers. Here we have found friends. Here I have found happiness. Perhaps this is the land we have been seeking, Damos."

Damos lifted his hand to silence him but Bendeguz also sprang to his feet now, aroused, the racking indecision and suspense of long months culminating in a burst of violent anger:

"Where, then, is Hadur?" he cried. "Why does He let this terrible hatred between brothers poison our souls?"

"Bendeguz!" whispered Damos in horror. "Are you like the Magyars who have lost faith? Do you, like them, shrink from suffering and death to gain that land? They will be punished for their weakness, Bendeguz. Long after the Huns have found the promised land, they will be still homeless wanderers in the wilderness. Some day they will follow your path but if they fall back now, if they choose the easier way, for seven generations will they roam the earth, outcasts among men. Your path leads westward, my White Eagle. Your path is the path of Hadur."

"My path!" cried Bendeguz. "Where is my path? Where is Hadur's guiding hand? Why is He silent?"

"You fool!" rang out the voice of Damos, and it was terrible to hear.

"How dare you challenge the wrath of your Lord? Go, before I strike you. Go! Call all the people together, to the altar. Light the fire! You will hear the voice, Bendeguz, and you will tremble and hide your face in shame and remorse. Go!"

Bendeguz looked at his pale face and a strange fear began to gnaw at his heart. He left the tent, walking in a daze. He gave orders to his heralds to call every one to the altar place to light the fires. Then he went to Alleeta.

She drew him to her and pointed a pale finger at the red eagle on the flag, spread to its full width on the folds of her tent.

"The red eagle, Bendeguz," she whispered. "It's moving . . . reaching out those cruel claws for me . . . I am afraid." He stroked her hot brow gently.

"It is but a painted flag, Alleeta. Do not be afraid, I will take it away."

"Take it, Bendeguz, or it will take me. And please stay with me . . . it is growing so dark . . . "

"I cannot stay now, Alleeta, but I will send a woman to you while I am gone," he said. She closed her eyes with a sigh. He stood for a moment looking down at her, then went away, carrying the flag.

The day had been breathlessly hot and now that night had fallen veils of heated mist rolled lazily in the air. The sky was dark, stars and moon were hidden behind slate-colored storm clouds. From the distance came the threatening rumble of thunder.

People were walking from all directions toward the altar where the fire was already burning brightly. Bendeguz drove the flagpole into the ground outside the tent, then he stopped a Cimmerian woman and told her to stay with Alleeta.

"Watch her—guard her," he was almost pleading. "She is ill and soon she will have a child. Do not leave her for a moment tonight."

When he reached the altar place, the great clearing was packed with people. At sight of the pale face and fierce burning eyes of Bendeguz, people fell back silently to make way for him. Damos was standing on the high altar step, in silent prayer. Hunor and Magyar stood side by side on a lower step. Men were feeding the fire with logs, women threw dry herbs on the flames.

Damos now turned. His face was stern and his sightless eyes as cold as ice.

"Bendeguz!" he called. "Bendeguz, whom I have named the White Eagle, face your people from this altar of your God and take back the words of doubt you have spoken before me."

Bendeguz was silent. He stood, his fists clenched at his sides, like an image carved of stone.

"Speak, Bendeguz!" cried Damos. "Are you afraid to face the scorn of your men—you, who were not afraid to challenge the wrath of Hadur?"

"I am not afraid!" roared the voice of Bendeguz. "I will repeat my words and not take them back. Men! Listen to me. If this is not the land we have been seeking, this sheltered land between two great rivers, why is Hadur silent? Why does He not guide us? I am not afraid of danger or suffering or death, but I want to know." He spun around, whipped out his sword and held it up to the sky:

"Here is Thy sword, Hadur! Turn it against my heart . . . strike me . . . but let my people see the truth!"

Only silence answered him. Menacing silence from the leaden sky above and a horrified silence from the people around him. He thrust his sword into the fire and stood defiantly, with arms folded, his angry eyes staring into the sky.

And then the storm broke. Suddenly, without warning it was upon them with lightning and thunder that roared and howled like an army of furious demons. Trees groaned and crashed to the ground to be picked up again and sucked into the spinning dark funnel of the whirlwind. Leaving a clean-cut broad path of destruction behind it, it was approaching the altar and people ran out of its way in terror. Bendeguz and Damos were carried along with the frenzied crowd out of the way of the howling spinning death. It struck the altar with an impact that sent stones crashing to the ground and swept the fire and sword swirling into the air. The sword was carried westward, two great tongues of flame streaming behind it like fiery red wings.

"The Red Eagle! The Red Eagle!" cried Bendeguz, and fought through the crowd to reach Alleeta's tent, a dreadful fear clutching his heart. No one noticed him now. They were watching in breathless silence as the sword flamed westward. Earth and sky shared the silence, as if all their forces had spent their strength in the storm. Then Damos the prophet was speaking again and his voice was like the tolling of great bells.

"Attila is born!" he cried. "Attila, with the mighty voice and wings red as blood. Attila, who will lead you into the promised land, the Red Eagle, greatest of all warriors, Attila."

A piercing scream rent the air and all eyes turned toward the tent of Alleeta. The woman, whom Bendeguz had left with his wife, ran toward him, her face deathly pale, her eyes streaming with tears.

"You have a man-child, Bendeguz, a mighty man-child—but Alleeta is dead."

PART FOUR

ATTILA

On a summer night in the year 408 a flaming red comet appeared over Europe striking terror into the hearts of all who saw it; a menacing omen, a flaming red comet shaped like a tremendous eagle with a sword in its talons.

In that year, when the walls of Rome were cracking before the onslaught of the Goths led by King Alaric; when the Vandals were invading Hispania led by King Gunderic; when Roman Britain was fighting a losing war against the terrible barbarian pirates, the Saxons—on a summer night of that year was Attila born.

And on that night did pity, tenderness, and love die forever in the heart of Bendeguz. The thousands who had heard his reckless challenge and had witnessed the dreadful punishment could and did shed tears of pity for him. The eyes of Bendeguz were dry, his face a cold mask, for the heart within him had turned to stone. He did not see the hand of Hunor held out to him with pity and love. He did not feel the restraining hand of Damos as he made his way once more to the now cold and dark altar.

He did not see that even the most reckless and ruthless of his men covered their eyes and fell to their knees when he again mounted the steps and lifted his face to the sky, when he uttered these words:

"Hadur, Powerful God, Thou hast indeed turned the sword against me, Thy sword, Hadur, not mine! But Thou hast given me a scourge in its place and I swear to Thee, I, Bendeguz the White Eagle, that I shall use that scourge, that I shall make it into the most dreadful weapon ever known to men. Thou hast given me a son, Hadur, he will be that scourge! My son, Attila the Red Eagle, the Scourge of God!"

And at that hour, Flavius Honorius, the Roman Emperor, gazed out of the window of his palace in Milan long and fearfully at the flaming red comet. He knew that the great structure of the Roman Empire was trembling and cracking under his feet . . . might this fearful omen herald the end? From afar came the sound of tolling church bells, from below came the sound of people praying in the streets and the droning voice of a friar:

"*Woe unto you! for ye build the sepulchres of the prophets, and your fathers killed them. . . . That the blood of all the prophets, which was shed from the foundation of the world, may be required of this generation . . . verily I say unto you, It shall be required of this generation.*"

"*And there shall be signs in the sun, and in the moon, and in the stars; and upon the earth distress of all nations, with perplexity; the sea and the waves roaring; men's hearts failing them for fear and for looking after those things which are coming on the earth: for the powers of heaven shall be shaken. . . .*"

At that hour Christians and pagans all over Europe prayed that this dreadful thing approaching from the East might be averted from them.

And in a dark tent, between the river Rha and the river Tanais, a new born child cried bitterly, cried for comfort and warmth and tender love, cried for the things he was never to know.

Early in the fall of that year in the month the Romans called September the great army of the Huns stood ready. It was night. Thick white mist hung close to the ground, but above, countless stars glittered in the dark blue sky. The full white moon looked down on what seemed to be the reflection of countless stars on the ocean of white mist: glittering tips of helmets, spears, and javelins, phalanx upon phalanx of them. The great army of the Huns was waiting, listening to the last words of old Magyar whom they were leaving forever. For the Magyars refused to go on farther, refused to follow Bendeguz whose face was stone, whose eyes were ice, and whose voice was like the lash of a whip.

The stars and the moon were listening too and the moon summoned a wisp of cloud to hide its face behind it. The glistening drops of water on the hard faces of warriors might have been drops of rain from that cloud, might have been the tears of the moon, might have been their own tears—who knows?

When the moon looked again, the sparkling helmets and spears were hidden in the rising mist. All the moon could see was the flag of the Red Eagle floating in the wind, moving slowly westward.

Slowly, very slowly, for the whole of Europe rose up in arms against that flag. More and more armies gathered to check, to stave off the implacable doom that poured out of Scythia. The fertile prairies, the plowed fields, and green pastures of Sarmatia became a battleground where a fresh field of glittering spears grew for each that death had mowed down, where brooks and rivers ran red with blood.

Sarmatians, Dacians, Goths, Franks, and Romans rallied in desperate effort to stop the Huns, in vain. Month after month, year after year, the Huns pressed forward gaining two victories for each minor defeat.

"They are not human!" spread the rumor in the camps of opposing armies. Survivors of battles and escaped prisoners whispered strange tales, tales which struck terror into the hearts of listeners. Tales about the man Bendeguz who knew no pity and would tolerate none; Bendeguz whose face was stone, whose eyes were ice, and who would ride into the most frightful slaughters always without a sword, without armor, carrying a small child on his shoulders. Later there were tales about Attila, the child, whose narrow slanting amber-colored eyes were like the eyes of an eagle, who, always in the van riding a coal-black horse, laughed at death, for death was powerless against him; Attila whose shrill voice rang out above the tumult of thousands like the scream of an eagle.

"The Huns call him the Red Eagle," ran the rumor far and wide, "and his father calls him Attila the Scourge of God."

"The Scourge of God!" echoed the cry from land to land.

"Flagellum Deii," whispered Pope Innocentius and sent his priests into far countries to preach Christianity with renewed zeal, to remind people of the words of the angry Lord:

"*The lion is come up from his thicket, and the destroyer of the Gentiles is on his way; he is gone forth from his place to make thy land desolate; and thy cities shall be laid waste without an inhabitant.*

"*For this gird you with sackcloth, lament and howl: for the fierce anger of the Lord is not turned back from us.*"

And indeed it seemed as if the Huns were superhuman. Joint armies of many nations became panic-stricken rabble, wrecked, scattered, trodden down to the dirt by this merciless avalanche of horsemen. The Huns themselves were like possessed fanatics in whose souls the vision of the promised land burned with such a blinding white flame that they could not even see the perils on their path. Their eyes were on Attila, Attila the fearless, Attila the invulnerable. They feared Bendeguz but they worshiped his child. To them he was a symbol—a promise fulfilled by Hadur—he was their great Red Eagle.

And the child Attila, who from the moment of his tragic birth had been deprived of love, tenderness, and comfort, grew hard as steel in body and soul. He had learned not to cry when he was but a few days old. Crying did not help, crying only brought a voice colder than the winds chilling his small body, sharper than the pangs of hunger. The only lullabies he had ever known were rousing war songs, battle-cries, and the whine of flying arrows. His only toys were sharp weapons and he soon learned not to cut himself, for if he did and whimpered with pain those icy eyes would freeze the whimpers in his throat.

He was hardly old enough to walk when he was strapped into the saddle and made to ride at the side of his father for long, weary hours. He had learned to handle bow and arrow before his speech had lost its childish lisp. His young muscles stretched, grew taut and strong, and if they sometimes ached almost unbearably no one ever knew it. The first words he learned were the thousand-times-repeated words of Bendeguz:

"Fear is sin. Weakness is sin." These words became his credo, a hard core around which he built his life.

Only after he had learned never to expect help or sympathy from anyone, did Bendeguz allow him to mingle with the men. Only then, listening to the tales and songs of the warriors, did he learn of the past of his people and of the future they believed in. And when he heard the story of that tragic night when he was born, a strange new feeling flooded his heart, love and compassion for this silent cold man who was his father. And a great determination surged up in him: to find that land, to find the sword of Hadur, to make the world kneel to its power.

From then on the child was a man, the Red Eagle who laughed at death. Death could not touch him, he had a promise to fulfill.

He was fifteen years old then. No one knew what had changed boy into man almost overnight, least of all Bendeguz. He only saw that Attila was taking more and more of the burdens of leadership on his own shoulders, that he held the tremendous army in a grip far stronger than his own had ever been. The way of the serpent was not the Huns' way they hated planned campaigns, feigned retreats, stealthy midnight attacks. Now, for Attila, they learned them all and scored more victories than ever before. They still loved the times best when Hun trumpets blared forth an open challenge to the enemy and Attila, clad in scarlet from head to foot, mounted on his coal-black steed, awesome like the god of war, led them into a whirlwind attack. Then indeed did they turn into demons tearing through the enemies' iron ranks as wind tears through a film of rain, demons roaring with laughter as the enemy scattered, scampering for the shelter of scrub and woods, a blood-speckled dust-covered herd trying to escape the doom of trampling hoofs and swinging swords.

At night after these thundering attacks they flaunted their wounds, made light of their losses, and roared their exultation in triumphant songs.

One night, after one of these sweeping victories, old Bendeguz went to

the tent of his son. Attila was asleep, his great body relaxed, a thin smile of triumph still lingering around his lips. Bendeguz stood for a long time looking down at him with a growing feeling of awe such as he had not known before. And then, for the night was cold, he removed his own cloak and laid it gently on his sleeping son. Attila stirred and Bendeguz left the tent quietly, puzzled at his own tender gesture.

He walked slowly to a near-by hill and up its gentle slope. The sleeping camp spread out below him and above stars trembled in the sky. He was alone in the misty night, seemingly in the center of the immense circle formed by starlit earth and star-spangled sky. Heaven and earth were silent, breathlessly, expectantly silent. And old Bendeguz, alone on the hill, alone with his God, sank slowly to his knees.

"Hadur," he sighed. "Mighty Hadur, I have kept my promise. I have made my son into the most dreadful weapon ever known to men. And now I am frightened at my own handiwork. Twenty years!" he cried, his voice suddenly loud. "Twenty years of war and millions of dead behind him . . . was it Thy will, Hadur? Will he ever wash himself clean of blood with the waters of the promised land?"

The cold stars trembled and the earth remained silent. But from above, from beyond the stars came a voice and at the sound of it the crust of ice suddenly melted from the heart of old Bendeguz. A voice sweet, soft, and so low that his ears did not hear it. He heard it with his heart.

Lead me westward,
White Eagle of the Moon, oh, lead me
On silvery rays of the Moon—
Westward I long to fly. . . .

Westward . . . always westward.

The wild mountains of Altain-Ula were but a legend to the Huns, the years by the misty blue lake only a fading memory. The past lived in songs, the present in their flashing swords, and the future in their hearts. The future was "a land between two great rivers, surrounded by mountains."

Mountains. But they did not know what mountains were. Since the tribe had left the blue lake their path had led through deserts, plains, prairies—flat or gently rolling land where their eagle eyes could sweep the blue horizon, where they could see the ponderous iron-clad armies of the enemy advancing slowly, where they always had the advantage over them, mounted as they were on swift prairie-bred horses.

And then, after half a century of warfare, when Attila was twenty-five years old, it seemed as if at last the great armies of Europe were exhausted. During the summer and fall of that year the Huns found less and less opposition. They were in eastern Dacia by late winter, having crossed the rivers Tyras (Dniester) and Pyretrus (Prut) at their lowest ebb.

Westward . . . thundering westward now like a wave lifting its crest. Warriors more than grains of sand or blades of grass on the plains. Under the hoofs of their horses the snow-covered frozen ground groaned and the icy air echoed with their shouts:

"Westward with Attila!"

Like a wave lifting its crest to hurl against a rock and fall back, its great power shattered into myriads of sparkling atoms, like a wave rushing on blindly, did they hurl themselves against a barrier, the great impassable sheer walls of the Carpathian Mountains.

Before them stretched the mountains in a tremendous arch, cliff upon cliff, peak upon peak, icy, formidable, without a visible break anywhere. And behind them, closing in slowly, confidently, like the jaws of a steel trap sure of its prey, came the enemy.

Day after day Attila sent out scouts to find a pass across the mountains. The men went without a murmur into the icy wilderness so strange to them where wolves howled and treacherous chasms waited for the unwary and those who returned at all returned with the words:

"There is no way across."

And listening to the deep rumble of the ground, watching the ring of campfires across the white plains drawing closer and closer every night, Attila knew that there was no way back. That steel trap fashioned with cunning and hate and the lust for revenge was closing in on them; it was more inexorable than the icy walls of the mountains.

For days the weather had been growing steadily colder. The sun was hiding behind leaden clouds heavy with snow. The Huns had no more wood for fires; the rocky cliffs around them were barren of trees. People huddled close together for a little warmth—silent, miserable, puzzled.

In the gray dusk of the seventh day Bendeguz and Attila were sitting alone in an icy tent. There was no need for words, there were no words to express what they felt. The impending doom of their people and their own helplessness tore at them with claws more vicious than the claws of the numbing cold. There was no hope in the heart of Attila, to him the future seemed darker than the thickening night.

Bendeguz was watching his son's face with a growing sense of apprehension. Those slanting amber-colored eagle eyes were mere slits now, slits through which he could see despair change into defiance and defiance into blazing fury. The sinewy hands of Attila were working, opening and clenching into terrible fists, and suddenly he was on his feet, his head thrown back, on his face a wretched semblance of a smile and his voice a tragic parody of laughter:

"The Red Eagle . . . look at me now, oh . . ."

"Attila!" snapped the voice of Bendeguz like the lash of a whip and his old eyes blazed again with an icy flame. "Attila, kill the snake of doubt in your soul, crush the worms of fear in your heart and mountains will move out of your way and your foes will become less than a handful of dust before your sword. Attila—pray, but do not challenge! Be strong, my son. Trust yourself and the God in your heart."

The tortured face of Attila relaxed. He laid his arm around the shoulders of Bendeguz.

"Forgive me, Father," he whispered. "Your faith is greater than mine."

"Yes, my son," sighed Bendeguz and his voice was heavy with memories, "it is, now." His steady gaze held the eyes of his son and a great, understanding silence fell upon them both.

Outside snow hissed against the tent and the wind moaned mournfully. Attila lifted his head.

"Listen, Father, listen to that wind. No!" he cried. "It is not the wind—people are calling my name. Listen . . ."

"Attila . . . Attila . . ." came the cry of many voices, "Attila!"

He tore the tentflap open and the wind smote him with violence. Dark shapes of men were tumbling through the tearing flood of snow.

"Attila," gasped the first to reach him, "LOOK!"

For a moment he could see only the mad swirl of snowflakes and then he saw, luminously white against the white of the snow, standing still like a majestic statue, glowing with an unearthly light . . . the White Stag.

Attila whipped around and swept a bugle from the tent.

"To saddle! To saddle!" blared the bugle above the howls of the gale, and others took up the call in the distance.

"Follow the Stag!" cried Attila, leaping into the saddle.

"Follow the Stag!" echoed the mountains.

"Follow the Stag!" howled the wind.

The White Stag moved ahead of them, now slowly, now swiftly, like a shimmering will-o'-the-wisp, always just within sight but never letting them nearer, leading them safely over treacherous icy expanses, across deep drifts of snow. Attila and Bendeguz were in the van, behind them the tremendous cavalcade breaking a path wide and safe for the pack-horses and wagons to follow. No one knew whither the miraculous Stag was leading them—the White Stag of Hun legends—the Stag of Hunor and Magyar. Perhaps it was their own faith they were following now as always, faith in the guiding hand of Hadur the Powerful God. Faith smoothed the path under the stumbling feet of their horses, faith gave them strength to ride through the buffeting wind and whirlpools of stinging snow into the unknown.

Gradually the storm abated. Ahead of them was still night but in the east the sky grew gray with waking light. And then they saw that the Stag had led them into a winding defile between towering peaks, a deep secret gorge eaten through the rocks by a rivulet. To the left and right were the overhanging cliffs, leaning over the gorge curiously like giants leaning down to watch a procession of ants. A faint green light hovered above the cliffs, then the pale golden rays of the rising sun poured into the gorge. The pass widened, rocks and cliffs drew back and gave way to gentle wooded slopes.

The White Stag was hardly visible now; in the golden daylight it seemed to have lost all substance and become light against light. Attila and Bendeguz reined in their horses and watched that shining radiance until it was no more. Then they drew aside waiting for those behind them to pass. For hours the immense cavalcade poured forth from the gorge flooding the sunlit westerly slopes of the mountains, winding like a giant dragon amid trees and scrub. The slopes were a billowing sea of spears and the excited voices of the multitude pulsed like the rushing of waves.

The sun reached its noonday height when the last heavy wagons arrived. After them the cavernous mouth of the gorge gaped empty; the Huns were across the barrier.

And on the other side of the Carpathians the blizzard raged for days. The east wind swept snow against the mountains like a gigantic broom, sweeping deep valleys in the snow on the ground, forming new ridges of drifts, covering the broken path of the Huns, and hiding, perhaps forever, the secret entrance to the pass.

"What enchanted land is this?" asked Attila of each golden dawn and every scarlet sunset as they advanced toward the west. The slim legs of his black steed fairly danced as he rode swiftly through the forest and field, his eyes scanning the ever-changing beauty of a land the like of which he had never seen before.

"What enchanted land is this," wondered old Bendeguz riding beside his son, "a land like an immense green bowl surrounded by mountains, warmed by the sun, sheltered from the cold?"

Behind them rolled the great army, their weapons and helmets glittering in the sunlight, in the moonlight.

"What enchanted land is this?" they thought as they rode through forests rich in game, across rivers alive with fish.

Spring had met them on the way and flung a glorious carpet of flowers under their feet as if spring were welcoming long-awaited friends. Winter and hostile armies were locked out by those gray rocky walls which had so miraculously opened to let them through. The few small tribes who inhabited this land showed no ill-will.

What enchanted land is this where new riches, new beauty, spread out before them every hour, riches and beauty cupped together under a laughing blue sky; where the joy of life and peace trembled in each opening bud; where the song of whispering breeze and gurgling brooks had the magic power to banish memories of bloodshed? Only seven days had passed since they had crossed the Carpathians and the despair of that stormy night seemed seven life-times away.

"A land, rich in game and green pastures, between two great rivers rich in fish, surrounded by mountains . . ." the legendary words of Nimrod chimed like bells of hope in the heart of Attila when, after crossing the river Pathissus, his swift-riding scouts returned and told him that within a day's journey to the west there was another wide river, the Danubius. He decided to let his people rest for a while.

All that day men and women worked joyously, happily, putting up tents, preparing for a great spring festival, a festival of thanksgiving to Hadur. They built an altar, the first altar to Hadur since they had left the Magyars. It was ready by sundown, a great altar carefully built; it stood like a monument of faith on the crest of a solitary hill above the rolling green plains.

Night fell, softly spreading its wings of silence over the sleeping camp. Sentry-fires glowed for a while then closed their eyes and only the stars, vigilant sentinels of the night, kept watch over the earth. They watched as the ghost-hour crept in among the tents trailing its mantle of dreams. They watched when, in the deep silence of the ghost-hour, a lone man, a tall majestic figure wrapped in a white cloak, walked slowly to the altar. The stars caught a glimpse of scarlet under the white cloak and they knew who the man was. They watched as the man before whose sword a continent trembled sank to his knees and touched his forehead to the cold stones. They listened and heard his prayers but the stars kept their silence, for it was not for them to answer.

Between the stars and the man, shadows passed on silent white wings; white herons returning from the south now that the long winter was over. They passed silently and when at last the man arose and lifted his eyes to the sky, the herons were gone. He only saw a single wispy white feather as it came drifting down, its edges pure silver in the starlight. It touched his upturned face and came to rest over his heart, and then he knew that his prayers had been heard and would be granted.

Before dawn people began to gather for the festival. They came afoot and on horseback from all directions, for the tribe was so numerous now that the forest of their tents stretched farther than eyes could see. Men, women, and children came bringing gifts to Hadur; single spring blossoms clutched in the tiny fists of babies, battleworn shields, jeweled swords and helmets, treasured possessions of old warriors. They came and laid their gifts around the altar, then joined the ever-growing crowd below the hill.

Old Bendeguz came, lighted the fire on the altar and stood waiting, his face turned toward the east where Attila's tent glowed like a giant red flower on the green grass. The dark sky behind the distant blue mountains grew luminous with the promise of sunrise. A murmur of admiration rose from the waiting crowd, for just as the first flaming arrow of the new day shot upward from the rising sun, they saw Attila riding toward them all red and gold against the glowing sky. His shining helmet caught the light behind him and it seemed as if he were wearing a golden crown. His amber-colored eyes looked straight ahead and the light in them matched the light of the sun.

There was no one among his people so silently watching his approach who would not have died a thousand deaths for him, their Red Eagle, greatest of all leaders. He was more than a leader, he was their king and he looked a god with the golden crown of the rising sun around his head.

A small girl tore her hand from her mother's fingers and ran toward Attila, toward all this shining glory, with outstretched arms. She ran, her little laughing face upturned, her small bare feet twinkling in the smooth grass. Attila dismounted and waited, smiling back at her, when the child stumbled and fell. She cried out and held up a bleeding hand to him and Attila, whose sword had dealt death to thousands, bent down to comfort the child.

Then, while he kneeled beside her, the sharp glint of metal caught his eyes, a curious, fiery glint. He reached for it, and his fingers closed on the hilt of a sword, deeply embedded in the soil. It gave to the pull of his mighty arm and he looked at it with a growing sense of awe. It was a Hun sword, straight and slim, and on the smooth surface of its blade was the chased image of a flying eagle.

His face grew pale. Holding the sword on the palms of his hands, he walked slowly up to the altar, blind to the crowd thronging around him, his eyes never leaving the face of his father. He saw that face grow as white as his own, he saw the strong lips tremble and he heard the hoarse choked whisper:

"The sword of Hadur."

The words echoed from the lips of thousands:

"The sword of Hadur."

Slowly he turned and laid one arm around the bent old shoulders of Bendeguz. In his right hand he held the sword and lifted it high above his head, pointing straight to the morning sky. His eagle eyes gazed unflinchingly into the sun and his voice rose triumphant like a bugle call of victory:

"Upon this altar of Hadur, our Powerful God, with His sword in my hand, I swear to Hadur above, to the Sun in the east, to the Moon in the west, I swear to the stars in the north and the stars in the south, to protect and hold this land against all powers on earth, for my people."

Then he mounted to the highest step of the altar and slashed the air with the sword—to east, to west, to north, to south, and stood again facing the sun, the rising flames of the fire behind him like great flaming wings, the sword in his upraised arm pointing to the sky. He stood, King of the Promised Land, Attila the Conqueror.